Space Cat

by Jeff Dinardo

illustrated by Ken Bowser

RED
CHAIR
· PRESS ·

Cat always dreamed of going into space.

Cat read many books.
She built many models.

Dog said, "Cats don't belong in space."
But Cat knew he was wrong.

Cat built a rocket in the yard.
It blasted off a few feet into the air.

But it fell to the ground.
"I told you," said Dog.

Cat read more books.
She built better models.

Dog said, "You are going to fail."
But Cat knew he was wrong.

Cat built a new rocket in the yard.
It took a long time.

Finally the rocket was finished.
Cat climbed inside.

Cat switched on the buttons.
She turned the dials.
The engines roared to life.

3....2.....1....blast off!
The rocket blasted off the ground.
It flew high into the air.

Cat had done it.
She was in space.
Cat was very happy!

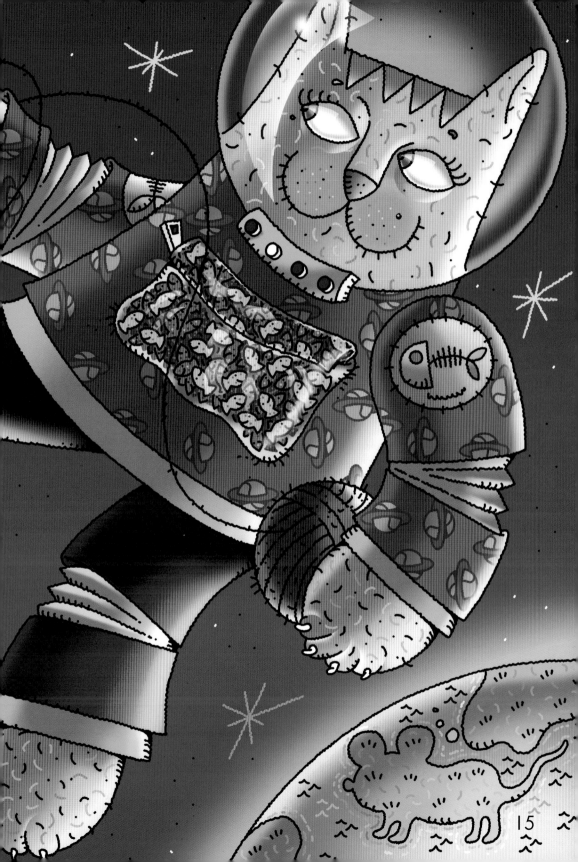

Big Question: Did Cat give up when her first rocket failed? What did she do?

Big Words:

engines: machines that make power into motion

rocket: something that can move high and far

space: the sky, where the moon and stars are